CRIMINAL

by

NADIA BARAKAT

PAGE PUBLISHING, INC.
New York, NY

First originally published by Page Publishing, Inc. 2016

ISBN 978-1-68348-050-1 (pbk)
ISBN 978-1-68348-051-8 (digital)

Printed in the United States of America

Harold Edward Styles wasn't like any boy.

He had a hold over the girls.

He didn't just take their breath away,

He also took their hearts.

That is 'til she,

Ariel Micheals, walked into his life.

She wasn't easily swooned.

She ignored his charm and witty remarks.

Ariel Micheals was a criminal in her own right.

She stole Harry Styles' heart.

CHAPTER
ONE

The alarm went off indicating that it's time for work at 7:00 am. I rose slowly so I don't get a headache. I was pretty tired since I stayed up talking to my best friend, Megan, about boys and boys and boys. It's like she had nothing else to talk about. I slowly walked to the bathroom, staring at myself in the mirror. Ugh. My dirty blonde hair was all over my head looking like a hat, there was some drool stuck on my olive complexion around my mouth. I had bags up to ass, since I didn't go to sleep 'til four this morning. My skin looked dead as I stared at it.

"Can't stand here all day," I muttered, turning on the shower. I honestly didn't want to do anything today. It was one of those Mondays that you didn't want to wake up to. Yeah, you know. I stripped off my Daffy Duck pajamas and hopped into the scalding hot water.

"Fuck! Why is it too hot?" I screamed but since I lived alone no one heard me. I adjusted the water to cool. Much better.

Sooner rather than later, I hopped out after brushing my teeth and washing my body and hair. I wrapped a towel around my body and headed off to my bedroom.

I stared down my uniform, hoping that I could change it.

It didn't work. I sighed loudly drying myself off. "Fuck!" I groaned as I put on the ugly grayish-looking shirt and the black dress pants that hugged my body. I had curves, but nothing to brag about. I was average. Probably boring but I was no Mary Sue, I'll tell you that. After putting my black gym shoes on, I decided to do my hair. I straightened the dirty blonde curls out. It was no use in trying to make it look good. I am going to wear that shitty Burger King hat. I hate it. I was debating to put on some makeup. I only put the black eye liner on, but not too much, just enough to cover up the hectic bags that resided under my eyes.

My cell phone rang just as I was about to leave the house and trudge to the bus stop. I don't have a car yet. Trying to save, but at the rate I'm getting paid, it would take me a fucking year.

"Hello?" I said annoyed, which was clearly evident in my voice.

"Woah. Don't get your panties in a twist, love." Oh, God, it was Louis. Sometimes Louis pissed me off. "Just called to let you know that you have training to do. We have a new guy. He's your type." Louis laughed loudly in my ear. How fucking annoying.

"Fine! I don't have a type. Dick." I hung up quickly. That jerk almost made me miss the bus. I hopped on the bus and took my seat.

Fucking three dollars for a fucking bus ride.

It should be free.

I know right.

Now, I was talking to myself. Great.

CHAPTER
TWO

Ugh!

The bus dragged on for about twenty minutes. Great, now I'm going to be late. Wonderful. I rolled my eyes and muttered a long string of profanities under my breath. I heard light chuckle and turned my head towards the sound. The person sitting behind me was in the same uniform as I was, but he wasn't wearing the hat. His hair was a mop of curls and his eyes were almost emerald. I narrowed my eyes at him and he immediately stopped.

"What's your problem?" I snapped. I hated that I didn't have any idea who he was. He stared at me with wide eyes.

"Nothing. I just…," he lowered his head.

"Good." I turned back around and the next thing I noticed was him sitting next to me.

"I mean, I figured you were upset." He smiled.

He has dimples? Somehow, I'm turned off. I sighed and ignored his other attempts at conversation. "*Yeah, this isn't going to work,*" I thought.

"Look, you look like a guy whom I can hate easily," I said rather bluntly. His mouth fell open.

"I haven't done a thing to you." He said a bit hurt.

Was this kid serious?

"You have," I countered.

"What?" He asked, a smile tugging at his lips. I swear he is trying to fuck with me. *"Why is he wearing the uniform anyway?"* I wondered.

"Why are you wearing that uniform?" I asked harshly, ignoring his question.

"Mhm...I'm going to be training," he said, pleased with himself. "Why?"

"Wh...What?" Is this the guy Louis was talking about? I hope not.

"Yeah, Louis said that a girl named Ariel would train me. He said she was pretty, but not his type."

Why that ass...Just because he's from England....

"Did he, now?" I asked. "Well, cause he said I was training the new guy." The guy's face froze. A smirk slowly spread across his face.

Millennium Avenue.

I jumped and so did that guy. He followed me all the way to Burger King's back entrance. Wonderful. I noted to myself.

"Hey, there you are..." He stopped. "So, you met Harry already?" Louis asked looking behind me and, lo and behold, there, standing tall...Damn, he was tall! He's making me feel slightly short. I am 5'8 anyway. I stared up at the cheeky bastard. "Well since you know each other, Ariel, you can show him the ropes." Louis just loved to piss me off. I growled as he turned his back on me.

"Look...Hansel—"

"Harry." He interrupted.

"That's what I said." I rolled my eyes. "We can start with the fryer." I looked at him. He nodded. We walked to the back. I wasn't surprised that the ladies were gawking at him with their mouth drooling open. I sighed and he chuckled.

"I have that effect on ladies." He winked at me.

"Except me." I added and he looked puzzled.

"Except you?" he asked.

"D-did I stutter?" I asked my own question. He laughed.

"Put on your hat." I barked. He did as he was told. Man, I can't stand him. I instructed him on the fryer and was surprised that he was doing an okay job. Not good but okay. Next, we started on flipping the patties and from there the drive through and then the front.

"Okay, you ass," I said in his face…not in his face, but that was the idea, it was more to his chest. "I don't care what you do or what you say, up front the customer is always right. No matter what. They can be wrong but they're right. No flirting. No nothing. Just take the order and send it through to the back through the register. Got it? Get it? Good."

Harry still looked puzzled as I told him what to do and expect. "Ugh. Watch me." I groaned and opened up the first cashier. The line developed as soon as it was open. Harry stood by me, watching with a fixed expression.

"Hello, welcome to Burger King. May I take your order?" I said in my best polite voice ever. The elderly man glanced at Harry then back to me.

"Yes, please," he said after a beat of hesitation. "One whopper, medium fries, and a large Pepsi to go," he said, clearing his throat. His eyes stayed focused on me, but every once in a while he would glance at Harry. I sighed.

"It's $10.50," I had to repeat it like several times. He gave me the exact amount and I gave him his receipt. We went through this routine until my shift was over. I showed him once again where to clock in and out. He nodded and did as I did.

"See ya, Harry. See ya, Ariel." Louis winked at me. Let me find out he did this on purpose. Just because I told him I had a crush on him when he first started, he's been teasing me ever since.

"Okay. Go home," I said sternly.

"Where are you from?" he asked, ignoring me as I walked in the dark to the bus stop.

"Here, born and raised." I stated proudly. "You?" I raised my eyebrow at him.

"Holmes Chapel." He smiled.

"Where's that?" I asked.

"England." Of course. I knew he was somewhere from Europe, but I would never have guessed. His English accent was heavy though.

"Ariel?" He asked after a heartbeat.

"What?" I answered as I paid my way and walked to the back with Harry on my heels.

"Nothing." He chuckled. We sat there in silence. That's the way I liked it.

CHAPTER
THREE

'm starting to feel like Harry is going to annoy me through the whole ride. Lucky for him, I have class and my stop is way before his. Harry started talking about something I could care less about. I zoned out and started thinking, "*Why the hell do I have to train him?*" Louis forced me into training him for three weeks on everything, to watch how he is with customers, and what not. I did not want to do this. I have come to hate Harry in less than the eight hours we worked together. My head hurts from working around him.

"Ariel?" Harry poked me. I glared at him angrily, might I add.

"What?" I said through pursed lips. He looked amused.

"What's your next stop?" *Is he really asking?*

"Milian Road!" The bus driver called. I pulled the string causing the bus to come to a sudden halt. I jerked forward trying to make my way to the doors.

"Bye, love. See you tomorrow." I didn't even bother to acknowledge his words. Man, oh man. Harry will be the reason of my death and not in a good way either. I sighed walking the night streets to my house. A sudden vibration startled me, making me rush home.

"It's my…phone." I laughed at myself and unlocked my door. "Hello," I answered.

"Hey!"

No, why is Louis calling me?

"I need a huge favor." I heard chuckling in the background. I groaned smacking all the lights on in the house and double checking to make sure everything is locked. Yay, no killer is coming to get me.

"You there?"

I sighed.

"Yes, Louis. I am still here. What favor do you need?" I said slowly trying to hide how annoyed I am.

"Tomorrow, Harry works in the morning and I really need you to come in. Please?" He begged. Louis knows I can't turn him down, but I have to.

"You work morning shifts. Why can't you?" I asked.

"Yeah, Louis, why can't you?" Some guy said with an accent different from that of Louis and Harry. *Am I on fucking speaker? Is Louis trying to piss me off?* I huffed and walked into my room to change.

"Louis. Take. Me. Off. Speaker." I replied.

"No can do. I'm driving." That-

"Call me when you aren't driving."

"No." That little-

"Fine. Fine. I'll work morning." I agreed.

"All day." I could see that smug smile on his face. I want to smack it right off.

"Fine!" My tolerance couldn't hold on to the little thread, so it came out.

"Jeez, thank you, Ariel." I hung up before I could say anything else that I would regret. I stripped my uniform off and put my sweats and a white shirt on. I threw my hair up into a messy bun. I was finished. I plopped on the couch and started flipping through the channels when a knock on the door came.

Fuck. It's a killer. Or worse, Louis. I shuddered at the thought. *It better not be Louis. I'll kick his ass. Actually, I won't but still.* I rose slowly with the remote in my hand and walked towards the door.

"Who is it?" I called through the door.

"Harry." *Harry? What the hell is he doing here?* I tapped my chin debating to let him in.

"Ariel!" He whined. I swung the door open and Harry stood there with a bag of taco bell and two drinks in his hand. Free food. I couldn't possibly turn it down.

"Enter." I told him. Happily, he obliged and walked in putting everything on the table. I noticed Harry too was wearing sweats with a black shirt and his hair was pushed back with…some kind of bandana.

"How the hell did you find out where I lived?" I asked after we had sat down on the couch. He laughed, passing me a burrito.

"It's. A. Secret." He smiled. He has dimples. I need to stop staring at him before I start developing Gulp feelings. I shook my head to get the image out.

"Louis." I started. He shook his head.

"Marissa. That hoe can't hold water to long." Harry laughed at that.

"Actually, Marissa and I had a date today," he said. My heart does a weird thing. *"Am I jealous? Hell, no. I don't care at all,"* I told myself.

"You're telling me because?" I asked taking a bite. Wow, this is good. I turned my attention somewhat back to Harry who was staring at me. "What?"

"Yeah, all she talks about is some guy called Derek. So I left her at McDonald's. Went to Taco Bell and grabbed a bite to eat. Then I remembered you," he said, disbelieving himself.

"Weird." I mutter. "The question goes back to my previous one."

"Can't say." He smiled showing off his dimples. "But I'm staying over."

I shook my head as I registered what he had said.

"No. You can't." He ignored me.

"You have an extra toothbrush. I left mine at home. My uniform is in the car." *Oh, gee sure.*

"Whatever." I said. I like to live alone, but this guy is barging in my life. Ugh!

CHAPTER FOUR

"Whatever." Harry didn't say anything. He just glanced at her before turning his attention back to whatever movie this was and his burrito, his second one in fact. He didn't see what her problem was at all. He just wanted to be friends with this uptight girl. Harry's eyes widened in shock. The reason she is so uptight was because she's a virgin.

"Excuse me?" Ariel said cocking her head to the side and glaring at him. "*She must glare on a daily basis.*" He shrugged mentally not wanting to upset her any further.

"Nothing." He said slowly.

"Thought so." She said turning her attentions to what was in front of her. The movie they were watching was so boring and the silence was unbearable. Harry could literally take a blade and slice through the tension. He looked over at Ariel. She wasn't bad, but she wasn't "oh my god hot" either. She was average pretty. Her dirty blonde hair fit perfectly with her grey eyes. She had curves in all the right places. Harry couldn't help but lick his lips.

"Take a picture." She snarled without looking at him. He laughed a throaty laugh. No one ever talked to him like that; he kind of liked it. Impossible. Harry didn't like her, just the fact that she is treating him like everyone else. That he liked. All the girls fawn over him. He didn't mind but sometimes it gets a little bit too much even for him. Harry sighed looking at his phone.

"Holy fuck." Harry said getting up quickly knocking the food on his lap off.

"What?" Ariel jumped up on the couch. Harry looked over at Ariel and laughed.

"What's so funny?" She growled. He shook his curls and laughed some more.

"You should see the look on your face." He said in between laughs and snorts. Ariel rolled her eyes at him. *Douche.* She thought.

"No. I have to go home." He said hesitantly. Honestly, he didn't want to go home. He was having a good time being normal with Ariel. Whoa! Harry had no feelings for this girl whatsoever.

"Okay, bye." She started to clean up their mess.

"Need help?" It wasn't a question. She didn't even bother to look at him.

"No." Was all she said. He helped anyway. She growled a few curse words under her breath but continued nonetheless and so did he.

Once they were finished, Harry still wasn't moving. This made Ariel pissed. "Okay, bye." She waved, annoyed at his presence.

"It's raining." Harry said looking out the window. Sure as hell is hot, it was raining.

"You have a car." She replied. Harry gave her a puppy dog look. "Bye."

Damn. No one has ever been unfazed. Harry thought.

"It's raining." He whimpered.

"Ugh! Fine, let's go." She said showing him the couch. "What?"

"What? The couch?" He asked, shocked.

"Duh. It's a one room." She put her hands on her hips.

"More reason to—"

"No." She then stalked off bringing back a pillow and a blanket and throwing it at him.

"Gee, thanks." Harry rolled his eyes.

CHAPTER
FIVE

"I sleep naked." Harry muttered. She rolled her eyes and headed to her bedroom. "Great, now I have to sleep on the couch," Harry groaned to himself. He couldn't believe he "The Harry Styles" has to sleep on the couch. Whenever he did spend the night at a girl's house, they let him sleep with them.

"*This girl is different.*" Harry shook the thought out his head. He has no feelings whatsoever for this girl. She hated him. He didn't know why but she did. Harry spread the blanket on the couch and threw the pillow with himself. The couch wasn't that bad. It was soft but not as soft as the bed would be. "*Would she be mad if Harry went into her bed with her?*" Harry grinned to himself and silently walked to her bed. He cracked the door open and heard her gently snoring. He smiled and walked into the room and made his way slowly into her bed. He beamed with pride at his success. "Made it," he whispered.

"Mhmm…" Harry froze. Crap. Shit. Fuck. Harry cursed. "I love you, Harry." She muttered, but Harry heard that clear as day. Harry didn't know how to respond. He thought she hated him.

"*It must be a different Harry,*" he thought. Since she hates him, she must have fallen asleep thinking about Harry…Henry…

Whoever that is but still, it couldn't possibly be him. He yawned and soon fell into the dark abyss of sleep.

The next day.

"Fucking Harry! Get the hell out of my bed!" Harry awoke to Ariel screaming her head off. He ignored her and turned over. "Are you naked?" She screamed making Harry laugh.

"I told you I sleep naked." He laughed.

"You didn't tell me shit!" She screamed. "Fuck you." She screamed and hopped out of bed, almost slipping on something. "Harry...boxers!" She screamed a line of curse words. She ran out the room.

Harry laughed getting up as well. He had gotten dressed and went to his car to get his uniform. Harry checked his phone after he and Ariel had gotten dressed in silence. It was 5:45 a.m. They had two whole hours before they had to get to work. He sighed heavily and started eating another bowl of cereal.

"You..."

"I'm not going to sleep here tonight." Harry interrupted her. "You snore and talk in your sleep." A grin appeared on his face as he watched her face fall to the ground.

"What?" She asked. Harry just shook his head not saying a word.

"Tell me." He shook his head again.

"I hate you." She said, angrily plopping on the couch next to Harry but not too close. She left a small space in between them.

"Do you?" She looked at Harry as he spoke. "Do you really hate me?" Harry smirked. She glared at him.

"I'll rinse the plate." Harry stood and walked to the kitchen. Harry smirked the whole way to the kitchen. He saw Ariel standing awkwardly by the door. "Need a ride?"

"If you had a car this whole time..." She trailed off.

"Sometimes my mum needs it." Harry said simply and walked out the door to his car. "Coming?" She walked over and sat in the passenger side not saying anything the whole ride there. Harry turned on the radio, which played Crazy in Love by Beyonce. Ariel glared at Harry for reasons unknown to him.

Once they made it to the Burger King, she flew out the car slamming the car door. Harry smiled and laughed the whole way.

This is fun. Harry laughed some more.

CHAPTER SIX

"That Harry," I grunted as I made my way to the kitchen where I'll be training him more. I let him sleepover once at my house and he gets all these weird kind of ideas. This is why I dislike him so much. And, to make it worse, I just met the guy. This day is going to end worse or what's worse than worse? Oh, yeah, horrible.

"Hey," I jumped at the sound of Louis's voice.

"Fucking Louis don't do that!" I screamed. He laughed. "What? I thought you would be gone."

"Well, well, look at you. Harry told me he slept over last night." I swallowed my spit and almost choked. Really? That curly-haired bastard.

"On the couch." I coughed. "He slept on the couch."

"He said he slept in the bed with you." Louis grinned. I don't know why he's grinning. Nothing happened between us. "He also said you talk in your sleep." With that, he left and Harry appeared right after him. As soon as Harry was close enough, I slapped him upside his head.

"Ow. What the fuck?" He looked at me.

"How could you tell Louis those lies?" I hissed in a whisper.

"Oh that." He smiled. "Oh that. Oh that! It was nothing."

"Harry, I hate you so much right now." His smile did not waiver like I thought it would have by now.

"Ah, Love, such a nice thing to have don't you think?" I glared at him and he continued. "When a girl talks in their sleep," I kicked him where the sun don't shine. He hissed in so much pain.

"Shut up, Harry. You don't know anything. I swear if you tell anyone, I will kill you myself." I whispered in his ear. I stepped back so he could fix himself and the next thing he did to me surprised the hell out of me. He kissed me. For a moment, the whole world stopped as his lips pressed against mine. No, no. This isn't happening at all. I pushed him away and he stumbled back. I was glad just the two of us were back here. Otherwise, people would start to talk.

"Usually, when I kiss a girl they want more." He said licking his lips.

"I'm not those kinds of girls." I spat and started the training making as little contact with this bastard. Honestly, it wasn't that hard.

Why did he kiss me? The question stayed on my mind even long after work when Harry walked me to his car and drove me home. Tomorrow, we were both off and I had nothing to do.

"Ariel, can I stay over tonight?" He asked me.

"Sure." I said without thinking.

CHAPTER SEVEN

"*Perfect.*" I thought after she had answered. Honestly I really didn't want to go back home. I didn't like my mum's new husband. He was a drunk, always beating and abusing her. My sister, Gemma, was always gone, so I really had no one to talk to about this. I just kept it bottled up inside me without telling a soul, but somehow I feel oddly comfortable around Ariel. I mean, if I wasn't, would I ask to spend the night…again? I think not. As we approached her house, I broke the silence.

"Thanks for letting me stay the night…again." I smiled weakly at her.

"Yeah." She huffed. She was so cute when she was angry. What? Cute? Where are these words coming from? I shuddered. That's fucking scary. I never thought a girl was too cute. I would never. Girls threw themselves at me on a regular basis. I mean I became so used to it that I didn't even care anymore. That is…no, that is nothing. Nothing.

"I need to go home and get some clothes then I'll come back." I promised. She just nodded heading out the car and slamming the door, I noted. Such an angry girl, yet I feel weird fluttery things in my stomach. It can't be love…can it? I never felt it…well, once when I was like fifteen and the girl just used me to take my virginity. That bitch. I'm glad I moved here with my mum, fucking Robin, and

Gemma. Robin honestly could have stayed behind. Before I knew it, I was at the familiar yet unwelcoming home on First Avenue. I hated this place so much that I tried to stay away. I turned the car off and walked into the house. I could hear muffled sobs from somewhere and another cursing and yelling about how his life would have been better.

The last time I tried to stop him I went to jail. I beat the shit out of him and my mum, my own fucking mum, called the police on me. She's lucky I still love her so much, otherwise…otherwise, nothing. I love her regardless. She's my mum. I sighed heading upstairs to gather some clothes and what not like my toothbrush. I grabbed a bunch of clothes from my dresser not caring if they aren't even folded and stuffed it in a backpack before slinging it over my shoulder. I made sure I grabbed my extra uniform then headed back out not before I heard Robin say, "Fuck you to hell! I need a drink!" Then I heard my mum's pleas. I sighed just standing there unsure what to do. Robin must have seen me when he rounded the corner because he froze.

"Oh, Harry," he said, remembering the ass pounding I gave him for landing a hand on my mum and Gemma. "Heading out." It wasn't a question, more of a statement.

I didn't say anything until my mum rounded that same corner.

"Hey, sweetie. Staying at your friend's tonight?" She smiled, but I could tell it was fake. I could see the tear streaks on her face. *Why does she let this man make her cry? Why is she still with him? No wonder Gemma ran off to college.*

"Yes, mum." I said to her and only her. "I'll see you Monday." She nodded knowing I'll be back whenever she called me if Robin did something to her.

Ariel Micheals' POV

That little…sexy…sexy? I was thinking Harry Styles was sexy. I must be losing my mind. Am I? I swear I am. If I am being honest with myself, I do find him a little bit cute. Okay, not cute. He's full blown hot! Yes. I admitted it. Harry Styles is hot as fuck. I wanted him to keep coming here. I miss his heavy British accent, I miss his hair, his laugh, I miss his dimples, and I miss everything about him. Love? It was too soon to tell if I loved him or not. I just…okay, I knew he was hot when I laid my eyes on him on the bus when he was talking to me. That day, I knew.

But, I won't tell him that. He will never know how I feel until I know how I feel. Love? Huh! It was just another four letter word. It had lots of meanings. Yeah, that's it. Lots of meanings. It can mean as a friend, stranger, family member, anything.

Or, lover.

Not as a lover. I. Do. Not. Love Harry Flipping Styles. I think it was just that he was hot and I was starting to have a headache from all this thinking. I mean I am way older than him. I'm twenty-two for crying out loud and he's like what…well? I don't know, but he's too young for me.

Age is just a factor.

This is really giving me a super headache. I need to lie down. Wait…Harry said he was coming back and that was like thirty minutes ago when he dropped my ass off. Oh, God. I miss that curly haired bastard. Just as I was thinking that, my doorbell rang. My heart leapt at the thought it could be Harry. Hopefully. No, not hopefully.

"What?" I swung the door open to find Harry, but not the usual happy-go-lucky Harry. No, this Harry was much different. Scarier, hurt, he was even bleeding and there was a lady standing next to him who looked like she could be his mom. I gulped. Something bad has happened. I don't know what it is, but it was something. He had a bag over his shoulder and was looking at the ground.

"Um…I mean come in." Harry didn't say anything. He just walked inside and, on the other hand, this lady just stood there.

"Hi, I'm Anne. Harry's mum. Can he stay here until further notice?" I could see the tear streaks on her face. Her eyes were red and blotchy and I could tell it took a lot of effort for her to keep smiling like that. I know it must hurt her face…a lot.

I nodded silently and she left with a car, which was parked right behind.

What the hell just happened?

I closed the door and turned my attention to Harry who was already cleaning himself up.

"What the hell is going on?" I asked him. He didn't say anything so I pushed it, taking a step closer to him, unsure of what he will do. When I came barely a few mere inches away, I noticed he was wrapping his hand with some black tape. "Harry, what's going on?" I asked, a little nicer this time. He looked up and smirked. His lip was busted. *Who…who did this? Is Harry in a gang or something?*

CHAPTER EIGHT

wanted to ask if he was in a gang, but was afraid to. It seemed he didn't want to talk about it, but I just couldn't let it go. "Harry," I said and he still didn't say a thing. *What the hell is going on?* I had to know. It was literally killing me inside. "Harry?" I asked.

"What?" He said annoyed and still not looking at me.

"Are you in a gang?" I asked him. He stared at me. I noticed bewilderment in his green eyes. He didn't say anything for a while, taking notice of my words that still lingered in the air above our heads.

"A gang?" He asked, a smile betraying his gorgeous features. *What? What the hell?* "You think I am in a gang?" He laughed. I mean the whole throw the head back, shoulders shaking laugh. I didn't see anything funny. I just had to know that I'm not harboring a fugitive in my small place. I waited for Harry to finish with his laugh. He finally slowed down and clutched at his sides.

"Are you done?" I asked, folding my arms over my chest. He nodded with a smile still plastered on his face.

"Yes, Love." He then winced at the sudden pain. I wouldn't be surprised if he was in lots of pain. He looks really bad. His usually curly chestnut hair is now all over his head, he had a purple bruise just below his eye and a busted lip. His knuckles were bruised or at least what I had gotten to see before he had covered it up.

"Looks like you're in pain." I mimic the smirk that was once on his face.

"Seems so." He says standing up the couch. We stared at each other for a moment too long. I was the first to look away. "I'm fine though. Since you're worried and all." *Is that sarcasm I hear in his voice? I must be hearing things.*

"Worried?" I asked staring in his green eyes. They were so perfect. A person could get lost in them. I mentally smacked myself for thinking this guy is hot. *What is my problem? I need to see a shrink. Yeah that's it. I'm going nuts.* I nod my head at the conclusion.

"Yeah, worried." He said in a valley girl voice. No, he did not.

Yes, he did, and with that sexy smirk.

Burn.

The voices in my head were having a war against me. That's the weird part. I sighed so loud that Harry started to laugh.

"Shut up will you. I am not worried. Honestly. I could care less." I told him turning my back towards him.

"Aw, if you weren't worried you wouldn't be asking if I was in a gang. Which, I am not by the way." He noted.

"I still don't care about you." I pouted like a child.

"Says the girl who lets me in her house every chance she gets."

"Baaaah!" I say sticking my tongue out at him. He laughed at me. I decided to change the topic. "Don't you work tomorrow?" I asked walking towards the kitchen. I'm pretty hungry and I'm guessing, so is he. Judging by the way he followed and was looking around the kitchen in search for food.

"No. Louis changed my schedule." He stated. "Tomorrow is my day off."

"Wait, Louis can't..." That son of a bitch. I could just hear him laughing at me. "So he told the manager to give you the same schedule as me." I say mostly to myself. Harry shrugs leaning on the counter top.

"What are you fixing anyway, sweetie?" I punch him in the shoulder and he winces in pain. I instantly feel guilty. Oh, shit. I just hurt him even worse.

"I'm So—"

"Kidding." He smiles at me. *That's not funny at all. This cheeky bastard, but on another thought, I don't think he was kidding.* "So, what are you fixing, sweetie?" Again with the sweetie.

"Don't fucking call me pet names." I sneer at him.

"Pet names?" he looks offended, but somehow it seemed fake. "Pet names are like a cat's name or some kind of animal. I call you sweet and innocent names." He explains. Really? Did he just try to school me?

"I'm too old for you to be calling me sick perverted names." I retort back.

"Sick? Perverted?" His mouth flies open. "You think I'm a pervert?" I nod. He puts his hand over his chest in attempt to be hurt. His acting skills are terrible. "I'm not a pervert…" He stops and then smiles inching towards me by the fridge, "…unless you want me to be." He winks, blowing his breath that smells like mint, on my neck. I push him away.

"Go somewhere." I huff trying to avoid how good that felt.

"Fine." He moves to the open fridge, where I'm standing, and he pulls out some ingredients.

"The hell you doing?" I ask him feeling like he is trying to take charge.

"Cooking. Duh, since you are taking forever Ms. Old Lady."

"You cook?" I ask, ignoring the name he just called me.

"Yes, Grandma. I cook." He's starting to piss me off. I noticed he took out all the things needed for tacos. Really? Tacos. "You like tacos or are they too hard for you to chew?" Old jokes. Funny. Not. Such an ass.

"Harry, Don't. Start." I huffed. I was starting to get angry now. These old jokes and this guy…

"I can't stop." Oh, god. No. Please. I like Miley Cyrus don't get me wrong, but I don't want to hear him singing one of my favorite songs in the kitchen while he's around my stove. Yes. Mine. Mine. Mine. "You're so red." He points out. No shit, Sherlock. I'm pissed.

"No. I'm just peachy as crumpets and tea."

"Ooh, a British joke. Not too bad, but not good either." He states, fixing the food.

"Didn't your mother ever tell you to respect your elders." His face dropped and I knew instantly I won.

"Actually she did, but you're ancient." That son of a bitch. If I leave the kitchen, he'll think he won. Fuck it.

"Just fix the shit." I tell him. which earned a laugh from him. It was low and throaty, which was hot as hell. No. It was ugly. Yes, very ugly, like this person staring at me.

CHAPTER
NINE

Her lame attempt at comebacks was very funny. I couldn't help, but laugh at her expense. I knew she knew I was laughing at her by the look on her face. She wasn't pleased. Anything I did didn't please her. "*Why am I trying to please her?*" I thought. I wasn't and it was the truth. I could care less for her, so why was I at her house and not someone else's. I shook my head working on the project in front of me. Tacos. My favorite. She watched me as I fixed the food in her kitchen. She just stood there staring. She wasn't even saying anything, which sort of freaked me out.

"So, are you in a gang?" She repeated. I thought I already answered this. I felt like I did.

"Yes. Ariel. I am in a gang." She gasped stepping closer. What's with this girl thinking I'm in a gang?

"Why?" She asked. I rolled my eyes not answering right away. I felt her grey eyes search my face. I didn't feel uncomfortable at all. Girls do this all the time, so why do I feel butterflies in my stomach.

"I was being sarcastic." I tell her, finishing up the food for the two of us. I didn't even ask if she could cook. I just took over her kitchen and she didn't say no. She continued to stare. "Ariel?" I called trying to divert the attention from me.

"So you aren't in a gang." It wasn't a question and I felt like she was talking to herself. I shook my head "no" anyway. "Good." She let out a breath that I don't think she realized she was holding. I smiled at her as I finished the food.

"Would you mind?" I asked not looking at her, but she was still watching me. She didn't say a thing. She just went ahead and sat the table in the kitchen. Now I'm going to be seated with her in the kitchen where there's no way my attention can stop wondering about her. I shook my head. Why would I think about her? I don't like her.

Love is a better word.

"No!" I shouted, causing Ariel to jump.

"No, what?' She asked.

"Nothing. Nothing." I said bringing the food to the table. I watched as she ate four tacos. She stopped and blushed as she caught me watching her. I smiled. I have never seen a girl eat like that. I'm glad she is comfortable to eat like that in front of me. Wait, no. No. I'm not attracted to her. I'm not. I swear.

"What?" She said with a mouth full of tacos. I smiled and looked away.

"Nothing." I decided to tell her what I was thinking. "I never saw a girl eat like that." She blushed a deep crimson red. I never saw her blush before. It's cute almost hot. My heart started to beat a tad bit faster. I looked away quickly.

"Well when the food is good, I eat a lot." I could feel her blushing, but I wasn't going to look at her and show her the blush that is creeping up my cheeks. I'm sure she can hear my heartbeat.

"You can sleep in my bed tonight." She whispered low, but I heard her. I took a quick look at her. Indeed, she was blushing and staring right at me. She didn't even look away.

"Um..., yeah that would be fine." I nodded my head. She smiled. Oh...she had the nicest smile ever. I think...no...it's not like that...ever.

"Well...I'll clean the kitchen since you cooked." She said standing up and clearing the empty dishes.

"Yeah, that's fine." I stood up and power walked to the living area. How long can I stay here without my heart beating out of control?

CHAPTER
TEN

cleaned the kitchen longer than usual. I wanted the awkwardness to stop. I never felt so awkward in my life. Not even when I was crushing on Louis. I can't even believe I offered to let him sleep in my bed. *What the hell is wrong with me?* I grabbed at my hair in frustration.

"Are you okay?" Harry poked his head in the kitchen. I nodded and turned back around the sink. "I was just asking because you were taking so long in here." I didn't say anything and eventually he left, or so I thought.

"This is crazy. I don't love him." I heard breathing next to me. I gulped. Oh, shit cakes.

"Love who?" Harry asked, staring in the empty sink. I turned my head in a different direction. How could I answer him? Or, I don't have to answer him at all. I can change the entire conversation. When I opened my mouth, my cell vibrated in my pocket. I held up a finger to Harry and he nodded.

"Hello." I answered, not looking at the caller ID.

"Hey, hey." It would be Louis on the other end of the phone. Wouldn't it? "Just calling to let you know, you and Harry are working tomorrow." He laughed. I already knew this. We were off for the holiday, so what is his deal? I listened to him some more before I hang up. "And?"

"And?"

"There is a new employee I would like you to train. Since you did such a great job with Harry, I would like you to train Liam!" I feel like Louis has taken his manager position just to hold it over my head.

"And he's your type."

"Louis, you said that about Harry!" I yelled in the phone forgetting that Harry was staring at me with a confused look. Louis chuckled before hanging up. I hissed at the cell phone in my hand and threw it on the counter top.

"So...," Harry started.

"I have to train the new guy." I told him and he perked up.

"New guy? Or new girl?" Harry said, staring at me without blinking.

"Guy. What's your problem?" I asked him before leaving the kitchen. I heard footsteps behind so I assumed he followed me.

"Just asking." Harry whispered, but I caught it. "It seems you only train guys and the guys you train get a higher rank than you." *Is he trying to piss me off?* He is right, but I don't care about manager or that. This is only until I save up enough to move away. Far away from Louis, Harry, Burger King, and the new guy called Liam. I ignored Harry's remark and turned the TV on. Britney Spears song Criminal was on, but I only caught a few words.

Momma, I'm in love with a criminal.

Why does that line stick with me? Harry hasn't stolen my heart at all.

"You know, I'll stay on the couch. I'll leave tomorrow after work." Harry said without looking at me. I didn't answer. I'm glad he's leaving. So why do I feel so sad? I looked at Harry who wasn't going to even try t make eye contact. That's fine. I'm okay that he's leaving tomorrow.

"Sure." I said absent-mindedly. I didn't want Harry to leave.

Wait. What the hell? I do want him to leave. I want him gone. I want my life back.

Harry then turned to me. "I'm going to head to bed early." I said without letting him speak. I changed into my pajamas and lay in my bed. I didn't sleep that night. My mind was racing at a hundred miles per minute. Harry was the only one I let stay in my apartment for this long. I wasn't in love.

Was I?

I couldn't be in love. Love was ruined for me. I failed in love. I came to the conclusion that it isn't meant for me. I am to be forever alone. But, why does my heart beat wildly when I mention his name or am just close to him? What the hell is wrong with me?

Maybe I am in love. I am in love there is no maybe to it. I am in love with Harry Styles and I can't help it.

He's not in love with you.

He's not. He probably couldn't stand me, He hated my guts for how mean I was to him. I deserve it though, but I had to know. I just had to know what he thinks of me. I decided to get out of the bed and see for myself. I would walk to the living room and act like I'm looking for something.

Perfect!

Easier said than done. I was pacing around my room debating if I should go or not. I paced for a good hour or so. I looked at the time and it was 9:30 p.m. I smacked myself and opened the door. I heard the TV so I assumed he's up still. I eased my way to the living room to see a mop of curly hair in his hands. He didn't even look up when I sat on the couch. "Do you like me?" Harry asked suddenly. I froze. *What kind of question is that?*

Of course. I love you, stupid.

But I couldn't tell him that. Or could I? I was just too afraid to admit my feelings to him, so I played the dumb role. "What do you mean?" I asked.

He looked at me sideways. He looked as if he has been crying. "How do you feel about me?" he asked. His voice was huskier than usual. He has been crying but why?

"Have you been crying?" I asked, avoiding the question all together.

"Answer me first." He told me.

How can I say this?
Yes, Harry, I have been in love with you since I trained you.
No, I can't say that!

CHAPTER
ELEVEN

How can I say this?
Yes, Harry, I love you.
I want you.

Yeah, that's not gonna happen. I can't tell Harry my true feelings. He will think I'm a freak and run away from me. I don't want that. I love him and want to keep him as close as possible. Woah, where the hell did that come from? I mentally shook my head. No, I will never tell Harry that I—

"Ariel, how do you feel about me?" He asked sitting up all together.

"How do you feel about me?" I asked. Before I say anything, I have to know how he feels.

"Well, you stole my heart and I don't want it back." My mouth fell open wide. Harry loves me. No, that must have been something else in my head, wanting him to say that.

"Uhm, what?" I asked rubbing my ear with my index finger. He didn't say that at all.

"I said you stole my heart and I do not want it back." he smiled.

Oh, fuck shit crap.

"Which means?" I played the dumb role.

"I love you. You are so precious to me. I don't know why I didn't see it earlier. Ariel, you're my everything." This is a dream. That's it. It's a dream. A very delicious dream that I love so much.

"Harry," I might as well tell him since it's a dream anyway. "I love you, too." Now I wake up. 1…2…3…Wake up. Wake up! Wake the fuck up! Why am I not waking up? I looked at Harry and he had a big Kool-aid smile on his face. This…this isn't a dream?

"Really? Ariel, that makes me so happy I can kiss you." And that he did and I still wasn't waking up. What is wrong with this picture? Oh, right. This is a hundred percent real and not a dream. No, this isn't a dream. This is something more. Something so weird and fucked up that it's so real. I shook my head and then started hitting myself with the palm of my hand. "Ariel, what's wrong?"

"I thought I could wake myself up."

"From?"

'This dream." I said stupidly, looking at the hurt expression on his face.

"This isn't a dream. This is real." I knew he would say that. Harry looked really hurt. I didn't mean to. I really do love him. He's perfect and different from all the other guys. Why did I have to say it was a dream?

Cause you are a heartless bitch.

I'm sorry.

Don't tell me that. Tell Harry.

"Harry," I just had a very short conversation with my inner voice. "I am so sorry. I didn't mean to hurt you. I do love you. I loved you since I met you. Harry, I didn't mean to hurt you."

"Then why would you ask if it was a dream?"

"It feels like that." I told him. I didn't want him to cry, so I took his head and held it to my chest.

"What the hell are you doing?" He asked not moving.

"Uhm…Isn't this what they do in relationships?" I asked, hoping that this was a relationship.

"So you are accepting the fact that you are now my girlfriend?" I could feel his smile on my chest. Is this supposed to make me feel horny? Cause it does.

"Yes, Harry. I would love to be your girlfriend." I smiled. Harry chuckled. I felt the vibration on my chest. I could also feel him turning his head and staring at my face. I looked down and oh, hot damn, he was fucking gorgeous! How have I not noticed how amazing this guy looked? It was as if God himself made Harry to perfection. My heart was going nuts. My heart never went nuts not even for Louis Tomlinson, the Don caster gangster. Never!

CHAPTER
TWELVE

What a crazy dream I had last night. It seemed as if Harry and I shared a moment. I shook my head from the dream, or nightmare, I had. I couldn't tell which it was. I turned my head to the side and there was Harry. I smiled at his sleeping figure then turned my back to him. Wait…Pause. Harry Styles is in my bed. Harry is in my bed. Holy shit! "Get the fuck up!" I screamed, startling Harry who gave me a puzzled look.

"What's wrong with you?" He asked wiping the sleep from his eyes. Last night didn't happen. It didn't. Oh God, How I hoped it didn't happen. "We didn't do anything if that's what you're worried about." He was still giving me a weird look. As soon as I opened my mouth, my phone rang. I held a finger up to Harry who rolled his eyes and lay back down with a huff.

"Hello?" I answered.

"You must have had a good time with Harry last night." It was Louis. *Was I late for work or what?*

"What are you talking about?" I asked confused. I didn't even bother to look at Harry.

"I mean you and Harry are late and I told you that you have to train the new guy today. Lucky for you, he is your type and he isn't here yet." Oh, shit. I did forget about work today. It's that stupid dream I had. It felt so real,

"You said that about Harry too." I sighed.

"Was I wrong?" I swear I heard him chuckle. Was he wrong or was I? Am I trying to deny my feelings for the boy I love? Do I love him? Was that a dream? I hung the phone up not bothering to answer him. He knew he wasn't, but I was in denial. Why did I keep denying my feelings?

"Harry, we are late." I told him touching his shoulder. I felt an electric shock and quickly took my hand back. Harry turned his head slightly to me.

"Not going." He mumbled.

"Why not?" I asked.

"Because my girlfriend thinks last night was a dream." He had a girlfriend? Why didn't I know? Of course, a guy like Harry would have a girlfriend equally as hot as he was. I stood out of the bed walking to the shower when I felt a hand on my waist.

"You can't be serious." He turned me around and his green eyes pierced my gray ones. "You really don't remember what happened last night between us?"

I looked at him confused. Wait, did I drink? No. I would've had a headache, so what was he talking about? He sighed, running his hands through his hair.

"Ariel, last night I asked you to be my girlfriend and you said yes." He had a small smile on his face. His perfect face. Wait, that actually happened?

"Oh, that actually happened?" He nodded. "I thought it was a dream." I told him truthfully. He let out a chuckle.

"It happened." he said pulling me into the shower. "I have this strange feeling that you are a virgin." He said taking off his boxes and throwing them on my face. I heard him give a low laugh. What a jerk face. I pulled them off and he was gone. I prayed silently he wasn't in the tub. He was right. I am a virgin. No one ever saw me naked. Ever. Not even on accident. I pulled my pajamas off and hopped in the tub.

"You're slow as hell." I should have known that he would be in here. Harry started to kiss me on my lips then he moved to my jaw line and nipped at my ear. I let out a squeal.

"Um…what are you doing?" I asked as he nipped on my neck, so that's how it felt. I guess Harry was doing it right because it felt amazing.

"Don't worry. I won't take your precious gift away." Harry mumbled in my neck. "That's for marriage blah blah." he smiled in my neck. His lips tickled and yet it felt so good.

"I…" I moaned as Harry continued to suck on my neck. I couldn't form a correct sentence, so I let him continue to suck at my neck.

"I want to do more, but we're going to be late." I nodded and held my head down. I too wanted more, but I'm not going to tell him that any time soon. We washed ourselves. Well, Harry washed himself and me. Somehow, he makes washing another up more erotic than it should be.

After we had gotten dressed, we headed off to work. I drifted off into my own thoughts. I didn't want Harry to go anywhere. He could stay with me. I guess I really didn't notice how it feels to be with another until Harry popped up. I like being with him, wait, no, I love being with him.

"Ariel, I don't want to leave." Harry said as he parked the car in the Burger King parking lot. "I mean if you want me to, I will leave." he looked at me with those sexy green eyes.

"You can stay as long as you want, Harry." I told him. He smiled and gave me a peck on the lips before heading out and opening my door. He helped me out. Out of the corner of my eye, I could see Louis smirking at us. *Am I going to get a lecture or does he want the details?* I shook my head. Harry grabbed my hand oblivious to the fact that Louis was watching us.

"Ariel, come here!" Louis yelled as we entered the restaurant. I told Harry about the training. He nodded and went to the back. "So, you and Harry huh?" He smirked.

"It shouldn't matter."

"Was I right?" He ignored me completely.

"Yes."

"Yes what?" He was messing with me this early. I swear he gets his kick out of all this.

"Yes, Louis, you were right as always." I rolled my eyes.

"Who's your best friend?" He was talking in a baby voice. I rolled my eyes and tried to walk away when he sidestepped me.

"Liam is waiting for you." He smiled.

"Okay." I said looking at him strangely.

"No cheating on Harry now, okay." He walked away from me with a smirk. Is Louis gay? It would be okay with me, but is he? He never said anything about a girl or boy, so does he hate people in general? Or, just me? Hm…I have to find out. I went to the back to find only one person there. He was sitting down, staring into space. He looked a little mature for his age, but nonetheless he was still easy to look at. Okay he was full blown hot. His hair was a fade, he had a little facial hair, and I could see visible tattoos. Harry had tattoos and so did Louis, so I guess that's okay. No one said it wasn't allowed.

"Are you going to stand there staring at me or are you going to introduce yourself?" He asked in a harsh tone. That attitude is a big turn off. "I guess I'll start." He sighed. "I'm Liam Payne. The new trainee and who the hell are you?" The nerve of this fucking guy. This is Liam. I have to train a delinquent. I can't. No. Louis has to find someone else.

"I'm training you then." I groaned loudly so he can see my displeasure in this as well.

"Great. A fucking woman." He threw his hands in the air. I wanted to wring his neck at this moment now.

"Let's go." I ignored him and walked out. He followed me complaining about the whole situation. I guess Louis told Harry to do something else. Harry and I are a couple. I'm so happy I can actually think that.

"What the hell are you fucking smiling about?" Liam asked.

"You have some fucking nerve acting all tough and British. I'm going to train you like I do all the new ones," I told him pressing random buttons on the cash register.

"Nerve? Women are the reason while I have the nerve. I hate your fucking species." I shook my head at how stupid he was. I didn't give a comeback. I just showed him how to do the register. He got it wrong all day. He was messing up until it was time to leave. "Well, babe, I see you can't train anything." He said squeezing my ass.

"You can't touch me." I said pushing him hard. I'm still not sure why Harry hasn't shown up yet.

"But I love you." Liam said trying to kiss me.

"Hey, what the hell do you think you're doing to my girl?" Harry yelled. Liam smirked and moved away with his hands up.

"See you around, babe." I smacked his hand away from my face. I love the way Harry said "my girl." Harry grabbed my hand and pulled me out of the place.

"Who the hell was that prick?" He asked angrily.

"The new guy." I told him.

"I don't like him." Harry said and I agreed. "You should quit." *Quit?*

"I'm not going to quit just because you don't like someone." I told him crossing my arms over my chest.

"Like tomorrow?" He wasn't listening to me.

"I said I'm not quitting." I told him my voice raising an octave. The car jerked to a stop and cars all around honked and cursed at us…more like, at Harry.

"Why not?" Harry asked. "We both agreed we don't like the new guy, so why not quit?"

"Because I don't run away from my problems. I will deal with this."

"While you're dealing with this, you can walk home." He said angrily.

"You can't be serious." H grabbed my bag, shoved it in my arms, and unlocked the door.

"I'm dead ass serious." He said.

"Fine. Have it your way." I opened the door and got out. As soon as I was out, he sped off and I started my walk home. That guy is a bitch. How could he? He better not come to my house. I'll slam the door in his fucking face.

CHAPTER
THIRTEEN

What am I doing? I just left her out there. She could get hurt, but I doubt she would even be where I dropped her off at.

I cover my hands with my face and curse to the sky.

Why am I such a fuck up? After all that confessing and whatnot the night before, I go and get highly upset over nothing. Nothing. I saw the whole thing and yet...

I drive around endlessly before actually pulling up to the house I so desperately wanted to avoid, but somehow I couldn't. I couldn't forget about her, that would be too easy. I sat on her driveway debating on what I should do. One side of my brain was telling me to stay in the car and the other one said go inside and apologize. The other side won. I turned the car off and headed up the steps to Ariel's small house. It may be small, but it's welcoming and warm. I shook my head as I lifted my arms, which felt like a ton of bricks at the moment and knocked on her door. I knocked for a good five minutes before remembering she had given me an extra key. I reached down in my pocket and grabbed the small key. Why was everything feeling heavy? Maybe it's because I'm such an ass that everything is weighing on me.

I unlocked the door and the house was dark. I had a very bad feeling about all this. She isn't here. Is what I was thinking? But before I could do anything, a cold hand covered my mouth. *What the hell is going on?*

"I finally caught you." This voice, wait, it doesn't sound familiar at all. I must not know this person. The person started to snicker and threw me to the ground. Hell no. I stood up quickly, wanting to charge, but I couldn't. *What the hell was happening to me? Did this ass drug me?*

"Ariel, you've gotten taller than I last remembered." It had to be a guy. Maybe an ex boyfriend, but he had an Irish accent. Oh hell, she does have a crazy ex boyfriend. I knew it. She looked like the type to have a crazy ex boyfriend too. My eyes were feeling heavy, but this douche was still talking.

"Babe, I don't know why you left me, but I've changed a lot. Just for you." Wait, I'm slow, there's no tape on my mouth.

"Ariel?" I saw the dark form of the guy stiffened.

"Who the hell are you and what are you doing in her house?" He asked, stomping over to me. Just as I was about to open my mouth and say some words, the door opened.

"Harry? And you?" She didn't sound too happy. I wonder, "*Can I pass out now?*"

"Babe!" The guy was tall, I'll give him that much. He was way taller than me. "I missed you." He tried to hug her and she dodged him walking over to me. She looked over me and made sure I was okay. When she was satisfied, she glared at her ex. I didn't hear the rest because I passed out. I will kick this guy's ass for whatever the hell he did to me.

CHAPTER
FOURTEEN

That bitch. I mentally cursed the boy that left me standing out in the dark. It was cold as hell out here and, to make matters worse, it was raining. Like seriously, Harry was being really pathetic. I walked to my house holding the stupid jacket closer to my body.

Why did he do that? I thought as I continued to walk down the endless night street. Cars honked but I ignored them. I wasn't going to look at these idiots and give them the satisfaction. There was one car that stopped by me, but I kept walking, not saying anything to whoever the creep was. The car slowly followed me and out the corner of my eye I saw the window roll down and sitting in the passenger seat was a familiar face.

"Need a ride?" Liam said with a grin plastered on his face. I stared at him for a good twenty seconds before saying something.

"Does it look like it?" I said putting my hands on my hip. He whistled and opened the door for me. I hopped in and gave him directions to my house. Once there, I hopped out and said, "You can't come in." Then I ran inside ignoring two cars parked there. Once I was in, I saw Siva manhandling a drunk-like Harry. I knew that bastard would have returned sooner or later. "Siva, what the hell!" I screamed and Harry dropped to the floor. Harry didn't even move. He just lay there, unmoving and mumbling. Something happened and Siva could have done it.

"Love." He smiled, reaching out to me. I backed away and ran to Harry. "Why do you always run from me?" He went on. "I love you so fucking much. You are my everything. Why, why? Why can't I have you?"

Siva screamed, glaring at Harry and I while taking out something from his pocket.

"If I can't have you, no one else can, especially him!"

"Harry." I whispered. "Please move." I eyed Siva out of the corner of my eye and he was loading a gun. I don't know what kind but it was a handgun. I tried to be brave to save Harry but he wasn't nudging.

"I gave him drugs, duh." Siva said, as if I should know this. I don't. I just got here.

"Harry, please." I whispered again. I tried to roll him over but he was much stronger and heavier than I. I had no idea he would be heavy. I grunted and tried again and then I heard a click. My head snapped in Siva's direction.

"Siva, please. Don't kill us." Siva laughed loudly with no humor, which scared me some. Okay, a lot.

"Kill the two of you. No, sweetie, just you." He grinned an evil grin making him look sinister.

"No, please." I begged. "What do you want from me?" I asked hoping he says nothing. Harry on the other hand was mumbling still. I couldn't make out the words.

"What do I want?" Siva tapped the gun to his chin making me flinch every time he did that. "Hmmm…I want you back." He said, slowly putting the gun down. I shook my head.

"Not in a million years." I sneered at him.

"I was hoping you would say that." The gun went off three or five times before it went black.

I love you, Harry.

CHAPTER
FIFTEEN

I love you, Harry.

When I came to, it was bright. Everything was bright and white. I tried to get up but then a sudden ache went through my body. Aw, what the hell happened? Once my eyes were adjusted to the bright room, I started to look around and saw that I was in a bed, not just any bed, but in a hospital bed. I shriek loudly and several nurses ran in the room with a panicked expression.

"What's wrong, Miss Micheals?" The blonde nurse asked. I was breathing hard and trying to figure out things at the same time.

"Where...where am I?" I croaked. My throat was dry. The nurse didn't answer right away but once she did, it was over.

"Well, you are in Saint Peterson Hospital. A young man brought you here. In fact, he stepped out to grab some food. He should be in any minute now." My face paled. Harry brought me here. I prayed that it was Harry and not that crazy ass Siva.

"What did he look like?" I croaked. I coughed to clear my throat.

"Um...He has curly hair and some tattoos on his arms. He's super attractive." The same blonde nurse finished with a dreamy sigh.

Yes. Harry did bring me here. Thank goodness. I let out a breath that I didn't know I was holding.

"Anything else, Miss?" The blonde nurse asked as she headed to the door. "I'll be back so you can take your medicine." I need to ask Harry what happened. I stared at the empty space in front of me, well; there was a TV in front of me playing Friends. I actually hated that show, just saying.

Some minutes later, a bunch of curls were in the doorway. I stared at it. Huh? And then, Harry popped his head in. "Hey." He whispered with a small smile on his lush lips. He walked over to the bed with a bag of Subway sandwiches. Hah. Frankly, I was tired of Burger King. Working there and everything. Harry must have been reading my mind because he said, "Yeah, I knew you would be tired of Burger King, working there and what not." I smiled at his thoughtfulness. Harry was so sweet to me. "Um…Louis and that guy Liam came over to check on you but you were asleep." Harry stepped closer to me, moving my dirty blonde hair from over my eyes, and then he gave me a kiss on the lips. "I'm glad you're okay."

"What happened?" I whispered softly. Harry's eyes started to shine with the coming of early tears. I waited for him to calm himself down.

"Well, when I came to and was able to move better, that guy shot you in the knees and in your arm." Harry said his fist clenched showing the white of his knuckles. "Two in your arms and three in your knees." He was shaken up about this, so I tried to drop it but he kept going. "When I find that pussy I'm going to kick his ass all the way back to his mother's womb." My eyes widened. I had never heard Harry threaten someone like that.

"Harry…" I started. "It's fine, really." Harry stared at me flabbergasted.

"It's not fine!" He yelled and I shrunk back. "He fucking shot you, Ariel. Shot you five times. That's not okay." He said rubbing the side of my face. "Your lips are swollen." Harry said absent-mindedly. Harry shook in anger. He was very upset. "Here, eat the Subway before they come back." Harry handed me the Subway. It was my favorite…What the hell is this? "It's a bunch of random things." Harry smiled sheepishly. I returned the smile.

"Um…" I started unwrapping the sandwich. "You shouldn't have." I said eyeing the generous offer Harry made for me. He was sweet but I'm not eating this. It had tuna, chicken breast, hot peppers, mayo, mustard, ketchup, Turkey, and other meat.

"I can get you something else. Louis said you like that kinda stuff." Harry was staring at it in a gross manner, now that I noticed. I knew Louis was behind this as usual.

CHAPTER
SIXTEEN

"That's okay, Harry." I said tossing the thing to the side. I really didn't want that nor was I hungry any more. Harry stared at me in an intense matter. He never stared at me like that. How long have we been dating?

He's going to break up with you.

Remember, he's a criminal. My inner thoughts were going crazy as hell. I didn't want to give into them, so I didn't. Harry continued to stare at me. I didn't want him to break up with me but his face says it all. I sighed softly, not wanting him to hear me. I turned my head back towards the TV to watch. What is that? Three old guys making bad jokes. I almost cried at how bad those jokes were.

"Ariel?" Harry finally said, titling my chin towards him. My eyes went everywhere but his green ones. "Can you look at me?" I did as he asked me to. He looked sad and I knew what that meant. He was going to break up with me. I had at least three boyfriends, one of them being Louis and the other being Siva and the other I won't mention at all in my whole life and Louis gave me that same look. Then he broke up with me. I looked at Harry trying to read his expression but he had on his poker face.

"Ariel I don't want to lose you but…" Here it comes. "But, I don't want to let that monkey fart win either. I want you. I never wanted someone in my whole entire life." What? That caught me off guard. I didn't expect Harry to say that to me. I'd expected something like "it's over bitch, go suck a dick." Or something like that, but this just caught me off guard. My mouth hung slightly open at his words.

"Really?" I asked feeling dumb as soon as the words left my lips. He nodded his head, still in poker face. "I mean you actually want to stay with me and not because you don't have anywhere else to go?" I whispered so low Harry once again had to lean close to me. I think he just wanted a reason to do so.

"I do have somewhere to go but you're way hotter and more fun to be with than the place I will be going to." He whispered just as equally low. I blushed. I mean full on blood boiling monitors going off blush. Harry stepped back with a satisfying grin on his face just as the blonde nurse ran in. She checked my vitals and everything.

"Don't scare me like that." She glared at Harry who was staring at the floor. "We called your parents and they are on their way. I know that you are 22, but still we had to do it." My mouth fell open. My parents? This must have been a lie. No, it's a bad dream. A very bad dream. My mom and dad, I haven't seen them since they kicked me out because I didn't want to become a fucking lawyer like them. I never told anyone this and now Harry will be asking questions. I can see it in his sparkling eyes. Wait, no, he's staring at a cookie in his hands. (Sorry, I tried to add to the joke about the way Harry's eyes sparkled when he's with Kendall Jenner. Any fans of hers, no offense. This is not personal. Keep reading. Thank you.)

"Um…." I tried and she took that as a good sign and left but not before a last warning look at Harry and her saying something about medicine. Fuck. Fuck. I don't want to go back to Great Valley Springs. I'm fine here with Harry. Harry looked at me with a question in his eyes.

"So um…your parents?" I nodded. "I just assumed they were dead." Harsh, but I don't blame him. I don't talk about myself much. I used to with Siva before he went crazy. "Wanna talk about it?" I shook my head not wanting to answer. "Okay, can you tell me about the whole Louis thing and Siva thing?" Fuck. Not now. I didn't say anything or even look at him. How could I tell him something like this? I can't.

He's going to leave you.

Don't tell him it's too much.

He loves you.

Oh, God, what do I do?

CHAPTER
SEVENTEEN

id I really ask that?

Do I want to know? Hell, yeah.

I wanted to know what was up with her and Louis so I can rest for just a little bit. Then I would ask what's up with Liam texting her. I needed all these answers.

"Harry," She sighed, lying in the hospital bed. I didn't like to see her like this but it wasn't my fault. It wasn't. I shook my head trying to get rid of the dark thoughts that haunt me. I miss my sister, Gemma, and my mom. I sighed knowing that I wouldn't be able to.

"Okay. Um...Harry," Once again, Ariel sighed, shaking me from my thoughts.

"Yes, Ariel?" I answered, staring into her deep grey eyes that held so much emotion that I couldn't read. She stared at me for a moment too long before sighing, and holding her head down, and letting her dirty blonde hair cover her face.

"Me and..." Did I really want to hear this story? Yes. Yes, the hell I did. "Louis and I used to date, but Siva ruined that one as well and so Louis and I broke up." That must be the short version.

"Did you love him?" I asked, well, whispered low enough for her to hear.

"Well, I thought I did." She admitted. "But I guess I didn't." She shrugged and stared up at me, waiting for my reply.

"Well. I guess that's enough." I smiled just in time for the nurse to come in with a big needle. Her eyes bulged out of her head.

"What the hell is that?" She screamed trying to get away from the needle like a cat trying to get away from a dog but it was trapped in the corner.

"No need to shout." The blonde nurse smiled and stepped closer to Ariel. She looked at me as if hinting to get out.

"No, he can stay." Ariel panicked. The nurse sighed.

"Fine. Bend over." This was strangely making me horny in a way. The needle was pointed towards Ariel, who was shaking her head at a rapid speed only seen in cartoons. Her dirty blonde hair went everywhere. The nurse was annoyed.

"Nu Uh!" Ariel shook her head some more.

"It'll just hurt a little bit. And you want to get out of here? So take this." The nurse put it closer to Ariel's thigh.

"It's going in my ass?" I had to burst into laughter at that moment. The nurse glared at me as I tried to cover it up with a cough, but that didn't work.

"No. Your thigh."

"Then why…" Before Ariel could finish her sentence, the nurse stuck it in her thigh. "Ouch, you son of a bitch. When I get outta here, I'm going to kick your ass." Ariel threatened. I shook my head trying to hide laughter. The nurse huffed and left. She must have to deal with this all day. I didn't feel bad for her though.

"You'll be fast asleep in an hour or so." She said and lingered by the door.

"Fuck off." Ariel huffed, annoyed. I kind of like this side of her. Unguarded and normal for once, instead of guarded and angry all the time.

An hour later, Ariel was awake. Well, as awake as one could be. She was getting drowsy by the minute. "What?" She yawned. I smiled.

"Go to sleep. I'll be right here." I told her. Before I finished, she was fast asleep. Louis came in with a bunch of roses.

"How come when I come in she is asleep?" It wasn't a question. Well I thought it wasn't a question.

"Well, the nurse gave her the medicine...so yeah." I said shrugging.

"Oh. When she wakes up, tell her to stay awake and I'll be here. I have to talk to her." Louis left before I could ask for what. My wanting to control everything started to come out.

Was I going to tell her about Louis coming?

Fuck no. She doesn't need to know.

CHAPTER
EIGHTEEN

I thought I heard Louis is here but once I opened my eyes not even Harry was here and my phone was sitting on the side table. Why is it there anyway? I stared at the spacious room with only the uncomfortable bed, side table, a curtain, and the television hanging off the wall. That thing could fall. The door creaked open and, for a moment, I thought it was Harry bringing me something. I miss him.

"Ariel?" The voice that wasn't Harry said and then he popped his head in. Louis. What was Louis doing here? Now that I recall, he was here wasn't he?

"Hey did Harry tell you I came?" Louis asked me with that smile I fell for.

"No. No he didn't tell me anything." I told him. His smile never faltered or anything. It just stayed there. Somehow, that was really creepy to look at, so I turned my attention to Friends playing on TV. I hate that show. It's so pointless. There is no plot, it's just there. Plus, Jennifer Aniston can't act then and she still can't act, and whoever said she was hot clearly needs glasses. I mean, no.

"Ariel, did you just wake up?" Louis asked, sitting in the chair that Harry had put there. I feel there is more to him coming here than asking random questions. I nodded my head. "That's good." He smiled and stared around the room in an uncomfortable manner.

"Louis, why are you here really?" I asked, wanting to know myself.

He took in a deep breath and then let it out. "I still love you. I know I made a mistake by letting your ex get in my head with the threats and everything. I love you. There's no one else for me." I wasn't ready to hear that, especially not from Louis's mouth. I blinked not once, but thrice. I couldn't believe my normal-sized ears. Louis just confessed. This boy that I once loved confessed how he still feels for me. "Ariel, please. Let me get another chance." Whoa. Pause. Another chance?

"Louis, I'm with Harry now. So you can't get another chance." I told him honestly.

"But you have Liam chasing after you." He harshly commented. "*First of all, Liam isn't chasing me*," I thought to myself.

"He isn't. And if he is, he will know that I'm with Harry." I said crossing my arms over my chest to end the discussion. Louis didn't get it, so he went on.

"He is. And, what will happen when Siva comes and harasses Harry too?" Louis asked. He doesn't know or if he does, he's acting like he doesn't.

"Louis, please. It already happened and Harry is still here, unlike you. Unlike you who left me on lovers' day." I told him turning my attention back to a condom commercial. Perfect timing. Not.

"You know he will come again." Louis whispered. I almost didn't catch it but glad I did.

"And Harry and I will still be going strong." I told him, not even bothering to look at him. How could he wish bad luck on Harry and me like that? I have enough problems.

"You think so?" He chuckled to himself staring down at his hands. "And when he fails, I'll be there waiting for you to crawl back to me." Louis said, forcing me to look at him. He yanked my chin up at him.

"Ow." I shriek in pain. "Louis, that hurts. What the hell is wrong with you?" I pushed his hand away. Louis looked hurt, crazed, and crazed again.

"Nothing. I just want you back. I even have my own place so we can be together and since we work in the same place, you know, or maybe even get married. I love you so much. I'm sorry. I'm sorry for everything I did to you. I'm such an ass." Louis said sitting back down in the chair. I kind of felt bad for him knowing his story and all, but still he should understand that I'm with Harry.

"You should understand that I am with Harry and I love him." I gave a small smile to Louis.

"You said you loved me too." Louis laughed coldly. Before I can say anything else to Louis, Harry came in empty-handed and stared at Louis in surprise. "Thanks for telling her to stay awake until I come here, mate." Louis smiled at him. We both know but I guess Harry is going to play along.

"Uh sure." He said looking between me and Louis. Louis left and that's when Harry bombarded me with questions.

"What did he say? Want me to kick his ass? Did he hurt you?" I lifted my hand up to stop him.

"Nothing, no, and no." Harry looked relieved.

"You know I will if he hurts you." He smiled. *Do I?* I guess the way he was trying to kill Liam. Liam? Whatever happened to him? As if on cue, Liam came waltzing through the door with a bag of food. Food? Yay. Harry glared at him as he made his way to me, opposite of Harry.

"Hey. How are you feeling?" Liam asked, smiling.

"Better. I'm just ready to get the hell out of here." Liam agreed. I saw that Liam had a tattoo peeking out off the collar of his shirt. Great, all the guys I hang around with have tattoos?

"I'll be glad when they release you also." Liam beamed. "I brought you a shit load of food. I have no idea what you like. And I wasn't bringing you Subway after hearing that they have been putting rubber yoga mats in the bread." *What? Ew, that's so gross. Why would they do that?* I stared at Harry who looked as if he could kill Liam for some odd reason, but Liam wasn't phased in the least it appeared. The testosterone is high in this room.

CHAPTER NINETEEN

"Well, now you came to see her, so leave" I stated finding him very annoying. I wanted to kick his ass. I hated this piece of shit. I watched as he smiled at me in a mocking way before talking to Ariel. *Who the hell does he think he is?* I was about to say something but then Ariel spoke up.

"So Um…Liam…" Clearly she was very awkward right now. I don't blame her I would be too but I'm not. Not at all.

"Yeah?" He offered.

"What are you going to do?" She asked. *Could she be any more vague?*

"Well I'm not sure. Maybe stop chasing after you since it appears I have no chance." He laughed. He is right and so honest and knows where he stands. "But as long as we can be friends, I'm all good." He smiled at her and she returned it. "And plus there's a new girl at work whom I've taken interest in."

"Oh yeah." Ariel smiled. "What's her name?"

"Danielle. She's amazing and beautiful. I think I may be in love. We only just started hanging out though, haha." He laughed awkwardly. Ariel looked at him as if understanding, which she didn't have a clue about. Just saying. "I think I should go." He left before any of us could say anything. Like I was going to tell him to stay and I'll be damned if Ariel was going to do that.

The hospital room she was in suddenly became quiet and tense. I was tensed and she was awkward. We didn't say anything about anything. The nurse came in, left, and repeated that action five more times before she decided to come in.

"Okay, Miss Micheals. You get to leave."

"Really." Ariel was bouncing with excitement.

The nurse did her job and left while Ariel was getting dressed. She made me promise not to look so I did listen until later though. I laughed to myself. After Ariel had gotten dressed and the nurse gave her the discharge papers, we went out to celebrate. Nice, fancy, except I made dinner at her house. After we did that and I cleaned the small house, we watched a really bad movie called Twilight. It was terrible but Ariel was enjoying herself. Some hours later, there was a knock at the door. I went to answer it so I don't have to watch this movie.

"The hell are you doing here?" I asked the person standing in front of me. I knew I should have ignored it. Fuck.

CHAPTER TWENTY

I t's been two weeks since I have gotten out the hospital and two weeks since Harry moved back with his mom. I don't know why Harry left but he did, and it's been two weeks since they came and stayed at my house because it was cheaper than a hotel and by cheaper it was free. I hated that word. On another note, Harry never told me why he left or said anything. He just packed up and left. I didn't know how to take this, so I figured it was a breakup but I didn't want to let him go. Harry was the only boy that stayed with me instead of leaving me for some unknown reason and he even stayed even when Siva intended to kill him instead of hurt me. I made a vow to find him. I would ask Louis at work tomorrow. My phone rang and, speaking of the bastard, it was Louis.

"About time?" He scoffed in the most playful tone ever.

"What?" I shot back not really in the mood for what Louis was planning today.

"Well, I was going to give you Harry's address, which is by the way 4343 West Hilary Lane, but I guess I'm not." I paused. Sometimes I love this guy.

"Is that all?' I asked knowing him.

"See you at work at seven morning shift sharp." He laughed and hung up. Louis is amazing, sometimes. I hopped in my car, put the address on my GPS, and drove all the way there, getting lost a few times and almost killing a human parasite and his idiot friend, and finally making it to Harry's house. I parked on the side of the street and debated what I was going to do. I decided and hopped out of the car and walked up to his front door. Just as I was about to knock on the door, he runs out with his fist bloodied and a guy on the ground, two women, one with blonde hair and one with black, crying. The one in black had a phone in her hands. I stared at the scene in front of me when the lady said something that sounded like "I'm calling the cops."

"You'll call them on your son? Fine. Fuck you and him." I never heard Harry like this before. It kind of scared me. He turned almost running into me. His dull green eyes coming to life as he saw me. We were quiet until the police sirens broke the silence. "Can I get a ride?" He asked and we rushed to my car. His mom...his mom called the...what the hell is going on? I didn't dare ask Harry while he was still shaking.

"Um..." I tried but failed.

"Can I go to your place? I don't care if your parents are there. I need somewhere to keep low."

"Sure. You know...I have a bigger place in the same area. It has two bedrooms now." I tried. He smiled a little bit and shook his head.

"Two bedrooms now?" He mocked me and that's how I knew playful Harry was back. "I didn't break up with you." He blurted. I didn't say anything. I swore he was reading my mind. "I just didn't want to start anything with your parents." I nodded understandingly.

Once in my house, my dumb ass parents started throwing questions at me. "Who's this?" "I don't approve." I ignored them and took Harry to my room.

"You just..." Harry started.

"Me and my parents never got along. I don't know why, I guess they hated me for the choices I made or whatever. But I don't regret any of them, especially you. I love you, Harry." I spilled most of my guts to him and he nodded but kept silent. As I was finishing cleaning up his fist, my mother, of all people, walked in.

"So, your boyfriend." It wasn't a question. I didn't say anything and eventually she left. Harry didn't comment and the two of us stayed in the room until I finished him up.

"Ariel, I love you too." Harry smiled kissing me, which led to more and some moans from me.

CHAPTER
TWENTY-ONE

It's been two weeks since Ariel has come out the hospital. It's been two weeks since I went back to my mum's house without saying a word to her. I wish I would have stayed but I couldn't. I felt I had to go. I hope she doesn't think I'm breaking up with her. Robin was awfully quiet and the house was quiet, too quiet, and it freaked me out a little bit. Mum was smiling and so was Gemma. I tried to shake it off, but I couldn't. I knew something was wrong when the phone rang and Robin flew his fat ass down the steps. I found myself wishing he hurt himself when he came down.

"Hello?" He answered out of breath. He needs to lose a few pounds. He paused for a lengthy moment and then in an inaudible voice said words. Once he was done, he flew back upstairs. My mom followed and soon there were screams and shouts. Gemma sighed.

"I'm so tired of mum and that twat always arguing. I wish mum would open her eyes and see him for what the hell he is instead of kicking you out over and over again." She was very tired looking and annoyed at the same time.

"You know, love blinds the idiots." She punched me and I shrugged. It's the truth, I wanted to say, but Gemma gave me a warning look so I shut up. Seconds later, mum came running down with a bruised face and a broken nose. My anger got the best of me and when I saw Robin coming down the stairs, I wailed on him. I continued to pound him. I ignored the screams of my mum and Gem. My vision was red. Red with rage. Red with anger. I just kept punching, whamming, and pounding. I didn't notice mum threw me off him, threatening to call the police.

"I'm going to call the police, Harry." Mum told me. My breathing was ragged.

"Mum...you can't, that's my brother, your son." Gemma screeched.

"I'm calling them. You have four minutes to leave."

"You're going to call the cops on me?" I asked. I turned around and was face to face with Ariel. She looked afraid of me. Of me. She must have seen something...or all of it.

"Can I go to your place?" I asked her. We ran to her car and on the way there, she was saying something and I said something. My head was hurting so bad I can't even remember what the hell was going on. When we made it to her new home that looked the same but bigger, we walked on and she ignored her parents. She fixed me up and then her mum came in, and was once again ignored. "I love you," was what I heard her say. After a few beats of silence I said I loved her too. I started the kiss and took it further to hear those delicious moans.

CHAPTER
TWENTY-TWO

Today was the day I finally go back to work and so did Harry. The uniform changed because Louis said so and blah weather and blah blah blah. So now, we were wearing a light blue top with the same black pants and gym shoes. I sighed as Harry drove up to the Burger King and parked in the employee parking that was new.

"What's wrong?" Harry noticed after I sighed for like the umpteenth time this last minute. Harry waited for a response.

"Just work…" I trailed off and Harry got the message.

"We can turn—"

"No. It's fine." I cut him off, opening the door, and walking with Harry on my tail inside where the AC was blasting cold ass air. It was freezing. I shivered and so did Harry. Louis who was super happy as usual for no reason came over and kissed me in the mouth for longer than he should. I was frozen. How could he? My eyes darted to Harry who looked as if he wanted to kill the guy kissing me. Louis finally moved back with a smile and then walked away. I was still frozen until Harry spoke up.

"What the hell was that?" Harry gestured towards where Louis had just left from wherever that was. We walked behind the counter and I started to set up the register for the day. Harry, however, was fuming.

"Harry. It's fine. I'm sure it meant nothing." Harry glared at me as if I was stupid. Was I missing something?

"Yeah and it's like if I trip and my lips magically smack into the person in front of me," he said sarcastically, with an eye roll and a scoff. "Stay away from Louis." My mouth fell open at his words.

"Louis is my friend and I will not stay away from him because you feel threatened. That isn't my fault."

"Still." Harry growled.

"Still nothing. Who put us together in the first place?" I asked him waiting for a favorable answer.

"Louis." He mumbled. I nodded and went back to what I was doing in the first place. Harry still wasn't pleased and I told him I loved him, which he didn't even say back.

I will not feed his ego because he wants to act like a stupid child. I huffed and waited for a customer to come. Finally, one did and ordered just fries. Just Fries? Nothing else. I sighed and slumped down on the counter. Today was the slowest day ever since I worked. Lunch came and ended, and then it was finally time to go home. Since Harry was my ride, I figured we'd ride together but I was wrong.

"I...uh...have to do something." He said and drove off. Not to mention, we do live together. The asshole. I didn't want to ask Louis for a ride, so I asked Liam. He was more than happy to give me a ride.

"It turns out that me and Danielle didn't get on well. And then she'd gotten fired." He informed me.

"Sorry to hear that." I told him, meaning it.

"Don't worry. So, you and Harry. Trouble?" That didn't even make sense but I totally understood it all.

"I guess so. He's been distant lately. Maybe it's time we end things here." I said more to myself than to him. He nodded his head and was silent for a few minutes.

"Well." He cleared his throat. "I would never treat you like that. I would treat you like a princess," he said, making me blush. Only three people ever made me blush him, him, and Harry. But it seems Harry would become a him as well. Sadly.

"Thank you, Liam." I said once by my new house. I gave him a kiss in the cheek but he turned his head so it could be on the lips. It lasted longer and was much better than Harry's kiss and his lips were softer and gentler. I pushed him back as much as I didn't want to I did. Liam was out of breath just as I was and had a look of emotion that I couldn't read. This felt right.

I don't know how but I knew something was starting right now.

My heart was still beating and I hurriedly got out the car but not before Liam spoke. "I love you." He said and then drove off. For once, I didn't have to say it first. For once, it felt right coming from Liam. For once, I didn't feel like a hopeless romantic. For once, I felt like Ariel. Ariel Micheals super star. Okay, scratch the super star, but I felt like me. I liked this feeling and ignoring the car beside Harry, I walked in.

I wish I hadn't seen what happened next. I wish I could have broken it off with him before it started. I wish I never met him. I wish I was Ariel Micheals before Harry Styles entered my life.

CHAPTER
TWENTY-THREE

After leaving Ariel, I quickly drove to the girl I have been having the best sex ever, Kendall, and went to her house. At that time, I didn't care about Ariel and what she would think. Sure, she was my girlfriend but Kendall had the moves and that's where I went. She may have been boring as hell but she knew how to put it down. She was good at everything from oral to you know. Of course, you do. Once I made it to Kendall's house she opened the door before I could even open it.

"Hey sex buddy. Here or yours?" She asked looking me up and down, licking her lips. I didn't want to do it here cause I think I saw her mom eyeing me greedily.

"The temp house I told you about with this bitch." Referring to Ariel as a bitch didn't sound right on my tongue but I didn't want to tell her she was my girlfriend and yet the words still sounded foreign in my head. "Take your car and follow me." I told her backing away and heading to my car. I waited 'til she gotten in her car and we drove to the house. I made a few stops on the way to get protection. No children running up in this place. I shuddered at the thought of snot nose kids running around. We made it. Lucky for me, she wasn't home. How would she be when I drove her? Well the lights weren't on, which was good. I hopped out the car and waited for Kendall who was being slow but whatever. As soon as the two of us were inside and the door closed, we started attacking each other. We ended up on the floor, naked and having sex, with protection of course.

So when Ariel walked in, I didn't notice. When she saw us, I didn't feel her eyes or anything. But when she spoke, I knew she was there and staring daggers at the two of us. Kendall covered herself up and stared at Ariel, who was beyond the healthy limits of pissed off.

"The fuck you bring a whore into my house and have sex with her on my floor naked!" She screamed.

"Um…" I didn't know what to say. I was there in a half-sitting, lying down position, with Kendall still under me, gaping and confused.

"Get out." Kendall grabbed her clothes and ran out. I don't blame her, if I could move I would, but I can't so I'm not. She glared at me and started shouting words I couldn't make out and they were all pretty angry words.

"I'm sorry?" I squeaked out a response and that led to how the men species of this time and age is so stupid and fucked up. I figured she hated the human species at the moment…well, men…or just everyone. She then started hitting me and I didn't stop her.

"Get the fuck out, Harry," She said with tears down her face. I dressed myself and did as I was told and left. I called Gemma and since she finally got her place, I asked to stay with her and she agreed.

Was Ariel and I over? Is this how it's going to end up? Would she go back to Louis or Siva or will she end up with Liam?

CHAPTER
TWENTY-FOUR

As soon as Gemma opened the door, she started bombarding me with questions. "What happened? Did you guys break up? Tell me! Tell me!" I sighed and sat on the couch.

"I don't know if we are over but...I cheated on her..." I trailed off and Gemma gave me a look of disbelief.

"Harry!" She shrieked. I thought she would have had another reaction than that. She stood in front of me, angry of course. "You never cheated on anyone ever!" She emphasized "ever." I let my head fall and sulk while yet another female gave me a lecture about how childish that was and what not. "Who did you cheat on her with?" Gemma asked crossing her arms over her chest.

"Um...that girl Kendall I had told you about some weeks ago..." I shrugged. I didn't bother looking up at my sister who was still beyond pissed the fuck off. It became deathly quiet after some time. I peeked up a little at Gemma and, yes, she was still there.

"Harry, how the fuck could you do that?" She huffed, stomping around. "She was the best damn thing that ever happened to you. Why did you decide to even get in a relationship if this was the out-come?" She asked.

"Because I fell in love with her." I blurted without thinking. Gemma softened up a bit and sat down next to me, putting her hand on my shoulder. I didn't look at her. I just kept my eyes focused on the wall. Once again, an uncomfortable silence fell over us. This was crazy.

"Did you tell her that…or did you leave things the way they were?" She asked with judgment clear in her voice.

"Left it." I mumbled.

"Why the hell…" She paused to take in a deep breath. "Why the hell did you leave it? Go. Fix. It." She said through clenched teeth.

"This can't be fixed." I told her standing up. "I screwed up. And this can't—"

"Fix it, Harold." I flinched at the use of my first name. She only used it when she was extra pissed off. I shuffled out the door and drove to Ariel's place.

I knocked on her door for a while and still no answer. I was there knocking for an hour when I saw Ariel come out the car with him. She knows how I feel about him. I watched as they exchanged conversation and whatever else. Then, the unspeakable happened. He. Kissed. Her. And she didn't even stop it.

I waited until she was barely at the front step before I shouted. "So, you and Liam?" I blurted giving her a shock. She clutched at her chest and I always wondered why women grab their boobs when they get scared.

"What the hell are you doing here?" She huffed, brushing past me to unlock her door. Of course, she changed the locks. I would, too.

"Well…" I began but was cut off.

"I made it clear that I didn't want you anymore." She hissed.

"You didn't!" I shouted. "If you did, I wouldn't have come back." I told her.

"Pfft."

"Ariel, I love you. I never loved someone as much as I love you. I fell for you. No one else. I know I cheated and that was a big mistake. I never meant to hurt you." I said and paused to try to catch my breath. "I wouldn't have gotten into a relationship if I didn't love you." Now I was finished and waited for her response.

"Mhm…I guess you're right. But you can still leave. I moved on. I like the single life." Those simple words shattered my heart. I couldn't let her go. That was too damn easy. I was going to fight for her. I wasn't letting no other asshole get her. I was gonna prove that I love her way more than anything.

CHAPTER
TWENTY-FIVE

Harry still hadn't left. He just stood there staring at me and I stared back. I already told him what I had to say, what more does he want? He cheated on me and that was it. I know he has been good to me but still, I draw the line at cheating.

Once a cheater always a cheater. I forgot who said that but it stuck with me. I tolerate most things in a relationship but cheating isn't one of them.

"Ariel." Harry's usually deep and wonderfully slow voice was now just a whisper. I had to strain to hear him. "We can't end things like this." He said, averting his gaze in some other direction.

"We can." I spoke monotonously, not giving away to all these crazy emotions. "You cheated. That does it for me." I told him. His gaze snapped and locked with mine. We stayed like that for so long. I can't even recall the minutes, hours, or seconds. So don't ask.

"Ariel, please." Harry stepped closer to me showing me emotion that I never seen in his dull green eyes that used to sparkle. "I need you. You're the only one I ever had such strong feelings for." Harry grabbed my shoulders and pressed me against his body. I could feel his heartbeat going at rapid speed. Somehow, it calmed the ruckus that was going inside my head and my heart.

If I'm honest with myself, I would say I still love this curly-haired bastard. I did fall for him. I fell harder than Justin Bieber's career and that's saying a lot.

"Harry." I didn't even try to push myself off him. I let my head stay on his chest and he didn't move either. "I…If I'm being honest with myself…" I paused and Harry started breathing a little faster than before. "I still love you." He stopped breathing for a moment then I felt tears on my face. I touched my face and it wasn't me crying, it was Harry.

"Give me a minute." He said. "I love you too and I can't…no I won't let you go. I will do anything to keep you. You're too special to me. You gave me hope, and love, and happiness. Before, I was just having sex for the fuck of it. I was with different girls every hour of the week. I never fucked the same girl twice but then you came and everything change. So please give me another chance to prove that you are the only girl for me. Please?" He held me away from him and looked in my eyes.

How could I say no to that? I thought.

Easy, just say it.

He poured his heart out to you. I thought these voices were gone but I guess not. I sighed and Harry waited patiently for me to talk.

"Okay, Harry." I said. "I'll give you one last chance but that whoever she is has to go." Harry nodded his head, his hair bobbing with it. He hugged me tightly and kept his word about proving I'm the only girl for him.

CHAPTER TWENTY-SIX

It has been seven months since Harry and I had that big of fight with each other. That night, we talked about it and decided that he is in fact a douche but lately he hasn't been one. In fact, he has been very sweet and kind to me. I actually like sweet Harry. He's so amazing.

"What are you staring at?" He smiled at me as we sat next to each other on the plane going to visit his mother who left Robin and went back home with Gemma. "*Good thing they didn't sell their house,*" I thought.

"Oh, nothing." I smiled at Harry and squeezed his hand tighter. He smiled back at me.

"Okay, so when you see my mum. Be polite and try to eat her food." Harry warned me. Somehow, I feel uneasy. It's really a problem for me to eat food from different countries. I'm glad Harry and his mom made their relationship better, but why would he say that about her food? Is it that bad? I waited for him to elaborate on it and he never did. Son of a...

"We are landing in the London airport. Please buckle up and do not stand either. I'm talking to you, Grandma. Have a nice time in England." Harry and I gave each other a look. As if to say what the fart?

"The fuck kind of…" Harry trailed off shaking his head as we got our luggage and carried it to the cab he held off. Our bags were put in the back and Harry gave the guy directions to his home in Chesire Holmes Chapel. It wasn't as far from England as I imagined but that's because I was asleep most of the time…so yeah… Anyway…

"Girlfriend." Harry kissed my forehead, helping me out.

"Boyfriend." I laughed as I grabbed his hand and walked with him to the front porch. I was nervous as hell.

What should I do? I asked the magic shell in my head.

Nothing. It replied. Okay, that wasn't much help and no more Spongebob Squarepants. I lied to myself. I offered to carry some of the bags and Harry slapped my hand and shook his head. A simple no need would have been nice. I pouted. It seemed like forever until we would get there but that's just nerves. Harry rung the doorbell and, seconds later, an overly cheerful blonde opened the door.

"Harold."

"Gemma."

"Who's this?" Blonde said.

"My baby," Harry beamed. Oh, goodie. Not. "Ariel." He beamed brightly.

"Oh. Oh!" She realized bringing us in and telling Harry to show me where I will sleep. He did tell me I will sleep with him.

Harry Styles

Night came a little too fast for the curly-haired boy who was anxiously waiting to spend most of his time with her but it didn't happen as he had envisioned. His mother and sister were all talking to her. Harry sighed in defeat. *The women in this house.* He let that thought go.

I'm glad I have my mum back. Was the thought that came next and he welcomed that once more. He loved his mum so much that it hurt for him to treat him like that. His mum was blinded by whatever he did to her but she's back. That's all that matters. His family is back with a plus one. His precious girl. He was going to show her around England in the morning.

"Baby," Harry called out.

"What?" Ariel said, looking at Harry who was waiting by the bottom of the step, waiting for her to come on over.

"Go on." Anne told her with a gentle smile on a face similar to Harry's. Ariel wondered who Gemma looks like. Ariel gave one last smile and walked over to Harry who ushered her upstairs and into his bedroom.

"So, in the morning, I have something planned." Harry smiled, getting naked. Ariel watched as he got undressed then she did the same. She knew Harry's eyes were on her and she liked that. A lot.

"So go to sleep." Harry pushed her down once she was in her pajama shorts and tank to match the floral print. Harry stayed naked…

The next morning

Harry showed her places she never heard of and they soon found themselves in Wolverhampton, West Midlands as Harry told her. Ariel was awestruck at how beautiful and sorta fun England could be. Ariel enjoyed herself until someone popped up and Harry's mood quickly changed.

Ariel Micheals

"Hey," Liam said with a smile and a hug. I returned the gesture and Harry was growling at this point. I didn't see anything wrong with what just happened. He's just being a dick. I didn't even pay him attention while Liam and I conversed. "I missed you back there in America but I had to come home. I missed it here more," Liam told me. I nodded understanding.

"Yeah. I'll miss it here too if I lived here. It's so gorgeous," I told him. He agreed and Harry was being a pissed off little baby. Seriously? It's not that serious.

"Well, since you two are having such a nice time with each other, why don't you hang out with each other?" Harry suggested. That was the first time he said something smart. Who knows when I will see him again? By him, I mean Liam.

"That's a great idea." Liam and I said together.

"Huh? I was being sarcastic." Harry all but shouted. He might as well have shouted instead of that gesturing thing he does.

"Harry, yes." I told him.

"No. And that's final." He said turning his back to me and starting to walk away.

"You're not the fucking boss of me, Harry. I don't see a ring on my finger." I told him and that stopped him.

"Let's go, Ariel." He hissed.

"No." I hissed back with more venom. Liam stepped back a little, waiting to put his two cents in.

"Um…tomorrow…"

"How about never?" Harry told him.

"Get over yourself. We are going to hang out and you are not going to tell me what to do. I'm a grown ass woman. You're not my father."

"I'm fucking glad I'm not your father. I would have given your ass up a long time ago." I was surprised. And with that said, he stormed off.

He left me. He fucking left me. I thought.

"We can hang out." Liam suggested and we did and, you know what, we had a good time too. Too bad Harry didn't come with us. Oh well.

CHAPTER
TWENTY-SEVEN

Today was the day Siva was done with the tour with whatever the hell band he was in. It didn't really matter cause four of them were not hot at all and only Siva mattered to me. Siva and I have been dating for five years and it's been the best five damn years of my life. I don't regret anything at all. Siva has supported me as I have supported him. He was there when my parents kicked me out of our sunny Florida home and sent me to a town I never heard of before. I had to find a place and Siva was there to help. Siva helped me 'til I found a job and still he wanted to help me then, but I declined.

"Babe, but I can help," he whined. I loved it when he whined.

"Siva, I have to do this on my own." I told him, sitting him down on the couch, and sitting myself down next to him. "You already bought this house. What more could I ask you for?" That was rhetorical.

"Mhm...Kids...Marriage. Me and you, forever." I laughed with him at his own joke.

These are the times I miss. The jokes, the stupid debates about which movie was better than which, why we shouldn't watch Spongebob at night, favorite bands, and etc. I miss those but, as the days grew shorter, he claims I have become more beautiful, over and over. He claims that guys are watching me more, which I doubt. He has been overprotective over me. I didn't like it.

"Where are you going?" Siva asked coming into this house that he had bought. I have been saving my money 'til I can get my own place.

"To work."

"How?" *Really? Did he just ask that?* I sighed with an eye roll and put my hands through my hair.

"I am tired this morning and I'm going to take the bus to work. Do not drive me or offer because I'd rather take the bus." He didn't say anything and I left it like that. It was like that for at least a week or so before Valentine's Day.

Siva and I didn't spend V-Day together, instead he broke up with me and I was not sad at all. I just kept doing me and saving for a better house for me.

I was proud of myself. I didn't need a man and I hate how movies say you do but you don't. I was happy single. The single life was for me. Just…myself.

I repeated it over and over.

ABOUT
THE AUTHOR

Nadia Barakat has four brothers. She is the only girl and the eldest.
She has always lived in the city of Chicago. At the age of ten, Nadia
began writing.

Printed in the USA
CPSIA information can be obtained
at www.ICGtesting.com
LVHW091336191023
761544LV00001B/260